# SCOOBY-DOO AND ALIENS, TOO!

Based on the screenplay
"Scooby-Doo and the Alien Invaders"
by Davis Doi and Lance Falk

Adapted by Gail Herman
Story by Davis Doi and Glenn Leopold

WORLDWIDE PUBLISHING
™

SCHOLASTIC INC.

New York   Toronto   London   Auckland   Sydney   Mexico City   New Delhi   Hong Kong

ISBN 0-439-17701-4

20 19 18 17 16 15                                        4 5 6/0

Special thanks to Duendes del Sur for interior illustrations.
Design by Peter Koblish

Printed in the U.S.A.

First Scholastic printing, October 2000

Scooby-Doo, Shaggy, and their friends were driving through the desert. The Mystery Machine's headlights lit the dark, empty road. Just up ahead, they could see a small town.

"All this driving is making me hungry," Shaggy said. "We need to stop for some chow."

But before they got any further, a strange humming noise filled the air. An eerie green glow lit the sky. It looked like an alien spaceship!

The ship hurtled past, sending the van into a spin — right into a cactus. The van's engine sputtered, then died. Fred, Velma, and Daphne decided to walk to town for help.

Walk across the desert? At night? Shaggy didn't think so. "Scoob and I will guard the Mystery Machine," he volunteered. After all, they could probably find some Scooby Snacks in the van.

After the others left, Shaggy and Scooby rooted around in the back, and there it was: the last box of Scooby Snacks!

Shaggy peered inside. "Like, there's only one left!" he exclaimed.

"Rhine!" said Scooby, grabbing at the snack.

The Scooby Snack flew through the air — right to a jackalope. The strange-looking animal scooped it up and disappeared down a hole. Shaggy and Scooby gazed down the opening. A green light shone from the spot — just like the spaceship glow!

"There's something creepy going on here," said Shaggy.

"Reel reepy," Scooby said calmly as he spied two glowing green aliens.

The buddies looked at each other. And then they screamed.

In a flash, Scooby and Shaggy raced to town. They found Velma, Fred, and Daphne at a diner, talking to the local townspeople about the strange ship. No one seemed surprised by what the two friends had seen. They'd all seen spaceships — and even aliens, just like Scooby and Shaggy.

Only Lester, an old man everyone thought was crazy, seemed interested in their story.

The Mystery Machine wouldn't be fixed for at least a day, so the gang camped out at Lester's house. The walls were covered with pictures of spaceships and aliens, all painted by Lester. Out one window, the gang could see giant satellite dishes.

"Those are S.A.L.F. dishes," Lester explained. "That stands for Search for Alien Life-forms. The government put them up to send and receive messages from space."

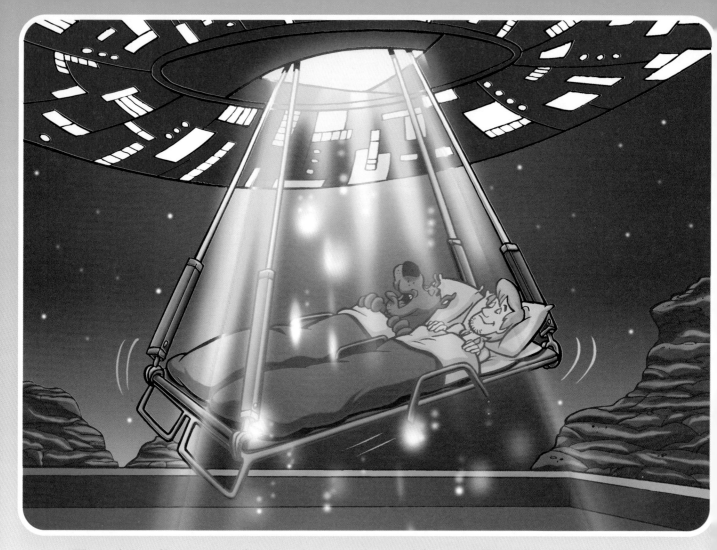

That night, Shaggy and Scooby slept on the roof in a couple of lawn chairs. They were sound asleep when a humming noise washed over the house. A glowing spaceship hovered above.

Shaggy stirred. "Like, turn out that night-light, Scoob," he muttered in his sleep.

Silently, four metal claws descended from the ship. The claws took hold of the buddies and lifted them inside the spaceship. Slowly, Shaggy opened his eyes. The aliens again! He and Scooby fainted, and all went black.

The next thing they knew, Shaggy and Scooby were flat on their backs in the middle of the desert.

"Hey, man, are you all right?" said a sweet-sounding voice. A pretty teenage girl and her dog were gazing down at them. The girl, Crystal, wore a necklace with a peace sign around her neck. She was dressed almost exactly like Shaggy.

"Like, hi," said Shaggy, already in love.

"Rello!" said Scooby. He felt the same way about Crystal's dog, Amber!

"I'm a photographer," Crystal told them. "Amber and I are taking pictures of wildlife."

"We saw a jackalope," Shaggy said, trying to impress her.

"Groovy!" said Crystal. She talked like Shaggy, too! "Anything else?"

"Raliens, roo!" Scooby put in.

Crystal's eyes opened wide. "Aliens, too?"

"You understand him!" Shaggy exclaimed. He was more in love than ever.

"So, can you show us where you saw the jackalope? *And* the aliens?" asked Crystal.

"Sure," said Shaggy. "But we've got to find our friends first."

Shaggy and Scooby piled into Crystal's Jeep. Shaggy pointed to the strange-looking equipment in the back. "You sure have a lot of stuff."

"It's my photography gear," Crystal explained. "Except for Amber's dog biscuits. Take one. Scooby will love — "

CHOMP! Shaggy took a giant bite.

"You're a riot!" Crystal laughed. Shaggy stared at her. She liked him, too!

Crystal drove Shaggy and Scooby to the diner, where they told their friends about Crystal and Amber — and the aliens.

"Shaggy must have imagined the whole thing," Fred told the others.

"But we all saw the spaceship," Daphne insisted. Something strange was happening for sure.

Just then the waitress came over. Shaggy shook his head. "Nothing for me."

"Re reither," said Scooby.

Instead of eating, Shaggy and Scooby hurried to the rest room to freshen up. When they finally came out, they stood straight and tall, with hair and fur combed neatly. That *was* strange!

"They are in LOVE!" Velma exclaimed.

The gang trooped to the town garage to check on the Mystery Machine. It still wasn't fixed, so they walked back out and bumped into Max, one of the S.A.L.F. scientists. He was going to the garage to buy oil for the satellite dishes — twenty cases.

"Hey!" Max said in a friendly way, introducing himself.

"Have you ever made contact with aliens?" Daphne asked.

"Not yet," Max said. "But do you want a tour of the station?"

"Could we?" asked Velma.

Were the aliens real or not? Maybe now they'd get some answers.

While Velma, Daphne, and Fred drove off with Max, Shaggy and Scooby headed to the desert. They wanted to show Crystal and Amber exactly where they'd seen the jackalope.

"Right rare," said Scooby, pointing to the spot.

"And then we chased it that way." Shaggy waved in the direction of a fence with a NO TRESPASSING sign on it.

"Zoinks! We didn't see that last night!"

Creepy shadows danced around giant rocks. A strong wind moaned, sending sand and dust swirling around the foursome. Crystal scooted over the fence. "Don't go in there," warned Shaggy. "That's where we saw the aliens."

"Come on, Shaggy," Crystal pleaded. "I want a shot of that jackalope. Pleeeease?"

Shaggy shrugged. He couldn't bear to disappoint Crystal. "Come on, old buddy," he said to Scooby. "The girls need us!"

Shaggy and Scooby led Crystal and Amber through beautiful rock formations. "Thanks for bringing us," Crystal said sweetly to Shaggy. She moved closer.

She really does like me! Shaggy thought. He closed his eyes, too embarrassed to look at Crystal as he asked, "Ummm, do you have a boyfriend?"

A deep voice answered, "As a matter of fact, I don't."

A mean-looking guard was standing in front of Shaggy!

"We're here taking wildlife photos," Crystal told the two guards. She was standing a few feet away now, taking a picture of an armadillo.

The first guard strode over and grabbed her camera. He snapped it open. Inside, there were tiny lights and buttons but no film.

The guard gazed at the strange camera, surprised. "It's digital," Crystal said quickly.

"This area is under government investigation for alien kidnapping," the guard said. "Now move out!"

The foursome quickly moved away. "I have a confession to make, Shaggy," Crystal whispered. "I'm not a photographer. Amber and I are government agents, here to see if the S.A.L.F. scientists are hiding any alien contacts. Will you help us? Show us where you saw the aliens!"

Shaggy and Scooby looked at each other. What could they do? They were in love!

A few minutes later, they led the girls to the spot. In daylight, they could see the hole was really the entrance to a cave. They stepped inside. But the guards were right behind them!

Suddenly, the guards stopped. Something that looked like a snake was slithering toward them, making a loud rattling sound. "Rattler!" cried one guard. Frightened, they hurried away.

"Far out," said Crystal, a little deeper in the cave. "Do that again, guys."

Shaggy made the rattling sound, and Scooby wiggled his tail along the ground.

But then, all at once, a real snake crawled over Shaggy's hand. "Ahhh!" he screamed, and everyone raced deeper into the cave.

Meanwhile, Velma, Fred, and Daphne met two other S.A.L.F. scientists — Steve and Laura. The station was so bright and clean! Velma couldn't help but wonder why the scientists' shoes were caked with mud. And all that motor oil Max had bought. Why, these machines used a different kind of oil!

Touring the station didn't answer questions, it just made Velma more curious. Why would the scientists need oil? Where did that mud come from? And was it all tied into the mysterious aliens?

A few minutes later, Lester picked them up. He was going to drop them off in the desert. After all, that was where it had all begun. There had to be more clues there!

"Do you think the scientists are up to something?" Daphne asked.

"I'd bet my teeth on it," Lester put in.

Fred gazed suspiciously at Lester. The old man was a little too interested in all this alien business. Then he noticed Lester's hands. They were green! Was it paint from all the pictures he'd painted — or from something else?

At that very moment, inside the cave, Shaggy spied a strange, green glow. The light came from a large chamber, just ahead. Taking a deep breath, Shaggy edged closer. Scooby, Crystal, and Amber inched along behind him. Slowly, they stepped into the glittering room.

"Gold!" cried Shaggy.

Jackhammers and equipment littered the floor. "I wonder who owns all this," said Shaggy.

"Raliens!" Scooby screeched.

"Aliens?" Shaggy repeated. "What would they want with gold?"

"Ask them," Crystal said, pointing to three green aliens.

Shaggy didn't stop to ask. He ran with the others — through chamber after chamber, tunnel after tunnel. They managed to lose the aliens. But now the guards were chasing them!

Not far away, the rest of the gang ducked inside the cave, trying to find the mysterious mud. They followed muddy tire tracks into a huge, cavernous room. A deep, dark pit as big as a canyon yawned open in the center. Then they spied a crane truck off to one side, and a giant net spread on the floor underneath them. Suddenly, the net lifted, taking Velma, Fred, and Daphne high up in the air.

"You should not have interfered!" shouted one alien, operating the controls of the crane truck.

"You can give up the alien act . . . " Velma said, " . . . Steve."

The scientist ripped off his mask. Max and Laura stepped into view, taking off their masks, too. Velma had already figured it out: The scientists had discovered gold while searching for sites to put the S.A.L.F. dishes. To make sure everyone stayed away, they dressed as aliens and

hired two friends as guards. They even disguised a helicopter as a spaceship and used it to kidnap local townspeople — *and* Shaggy and Scooby.

"You're pretty smart," Steve said to Velma. "Too bad you've made your last deduction." He pulled a lever, and the net swung crazily over the pit.

On the other side, the guards backed Shaggy, Scooby, Crystal, and Amber to the very edge. "Zoinks!" said Shaggy, gazing down. He and Scooby squared their shoulders, then stepped in front of the girls. No one would hurt Crystal and Amber. "Like, stand back!" Shaggy warned the guards. He struck a threatening pose. "We know . . . stuff!"

The guards snickered and moved forward.

Standing behind the buddies, Crystal and Amber looked at each other, then nodded. Then Crystal touched her peace sign. The medallion glowed, and suddenly, the girl and her dog were transformed into aliens, enormous aliens — and terrifyingly real!

The guards fled. Quickly, before Shaggy and Scooby could turn around and see, Crystal and Amber turned back to their earth forms. "You frightened them off!" Crystal exclaimed, hugging Shaggy.

All at once, screams echoed through the cavern. "Zoinks!" cried Shaggy. "It's the gang!"

They followed the shouts and raced up to the crane truck, where the guards were babbling to the scientists. "Aliens!" they cried.

No one was watching the prisoners in the net. Swinging dangerously back and forth, Velma, Fred, and Daphne began to climb out.

"There they are!" one guard said, pointing a shaky finger at Crystal and Amber.

Shaggy thought the guard was talking about him. "I see you need another lesson," he said.

Then, before anyone could move, one guard reached over and knocked down Shaggy and Scooby. The buddies sank to the floor, eyes closed. Furious, Crystal and Amber transformed once more.

"Jinkies!" Velma whispered. She gazed wide-eyed at the aliens as she, Daphne, and Fred jumped from the net onto the ground.

The guards screamed, then raced away — straight into a heavy metal beam. Amber grabbed the beam and twisted it tightly around the guards, trapping them in place.

The scientists took off, too. But Fred jumped to the control panel and pushed a lever.

"Yes!" he cried as the net swung over the scientists and dropped down over them neatly.

Crystal and Amber bent over Shaggy and Scooby. "Are you all right?" Crystal asked.

"Yeah," said Shaggy. He opened his eyes and saw the alien Crystal for the first time. "Ahhh!" he shouted.

"I have another confession," Crystal said. "We are government agents, but not from Earth. We were sent by our world to investigate signals from your planet."

"From the S.A.L.F. station," Amber added. She could talk, too!

"We learned about your planet from watching old TV transmissions," Crystal explained.

"Aha!" said Velma. "That's why you're dressed like that."

Suddenly, a light beamed down from above. It was the alien spaceship, the same one the gang had seen the other day.

"We have to go," Crystal said to Shaggy. "But can you forgive us for deceiving you?"

"Yeah." Shaggy nodded sadly. "Like, I understand."

"Ree, roo, Ramber," said Scooby.

They watched in silence as Crystal and Amber shrank into the light, then whooshed up into the spaceship. Moments later, they were gone.

The scientists and guards were arrested, and a few hours later the Mystery Machine was repaired. It was time for the gang to go.

Shaggy and Scooby climbed into the van, shoulders drooping.

"Like, we're destroyed," Shaggy said. "It will take us forever to get over Crystal and Amber."

"Reah," agreed Scooby. "Rorever."

Velma held up a box of Scooby Snacks. Shaggy and Scooby reached for it happily.

"Well," said Velma, "that didn't take too long after all!"